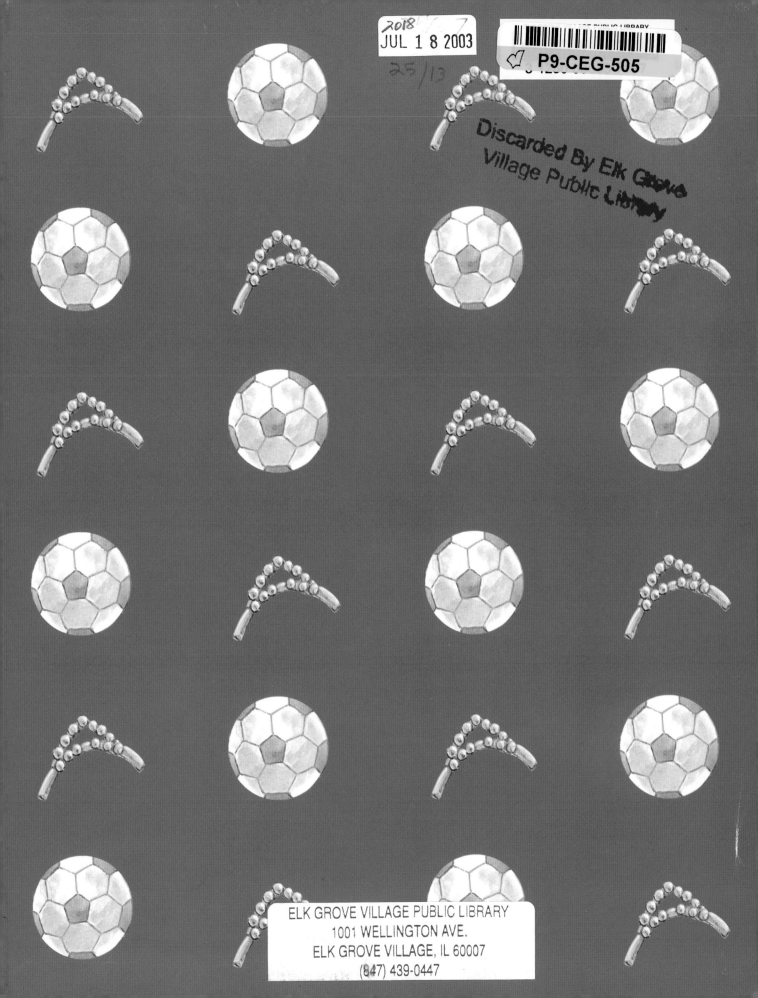

First published in Great Britain in 2003 by Brimax™,
an imprint of Octopus Publishing Group Ltd
2-4 Heron Quays, London E14 4JP

Text and illustrations copyright © Octopus Publishing Ltd 2003

Mc Graw Hill **Children's Publishing**

This edition published in the United States of America in 2003 by
Gingham Dog Press
an imprint of McGraw-Hill Children's Publishing,
a Division of The McGraw-Hill Companies
8787 Orion Place
Columbus, Ohio 43240-4027

www.MHkids.com

Library of Congress Cataloging-in-Publication Data is on file with the publisher.

Printed in China.

1-57768-447-8

1 2 3 4 5 6 7 8 9 10 BRI 09 08 07 06 05 04 03

The McGraw·Hill Companies

Princess Fidgety Feet

By Pat Posner

Illustrated by

Philip Norman

GINGHAM DOG PRESS

Columbus, Ohio

It was morning in the royal household and Princess Bridget was stuck eating cornflakes with her parents, the king and queen.

What she really wanted to do was go to the tower room and look through the telescope.

Princess Bridget liked the tower room because she could watch children playing soccer in the soccer field. The field was a long way from the castle, but looking through the telescope made everything seem much closer.

Princess Bridget secretly wanted to play soccer with the other children. She thought about it all the time, even when she was doing princessy things.

Things like dancing at the Royal Ball

or waving to her loyal subjects

or greeting important visitors

or watching an opera in
the Royal Box.

Every Thursday afternoon, her friend Ryan, the palace paperboy, played soccer in the park. Princess Bridget always watched him through the telescope. When Ryan kicked the ball, Princess Bridget imagined kicking the ball. When he scored a goal, she imagined scoring a goal, too.

When the soccer game ended, Princess Bridget waited for Ryan. She knew he would rush up to the tower room as soon as he finished delivering papers. Once he got there, Princess Bridget and Ryan played a quick game of soccer. It wasn't a princessy thing to do, so they had to be very quiet and keep their game a secret.

Little did they know that the king was in on the secret! He often climbed up to the tower room to watch them play. Princess Bridget and Ryan never noticed.

Back at the breakfast table, Princess Bridget ate her cornflakes and thought about the game she and Ryan had played yesterday. First her left foot jerked. Then her right foot jerked.

"Do keep still, Bridget," scolded the queen. "Princesses should not wriggle their feet at the table."

"But my feet want to move," Princess Bridget told her mother. "They want to run and jump and hop and leap."

"They should not want to run and jump and hop and leap *all* the time," said the queen with a sigh. "No wonder everyone calls you 'Princess Fidgety Feet.'"

The king peered at his daughter. "I'll send for Miss Posy," he said. "Miss Posy will know what to do about fidgety feet."

Word of Miss Posy's arrival spread quickly through the palace. That afternoon, Ryan sprinted up to the tower room.

"Who's Miss Posy?" he said, panting.

Princess Bridget clutched the soccer ball. "She's the one who's going to ruin my life!"

"How's she going to do that?" asked Ryan, his eyes wide.

"She's going to stop my feet from fidgeting," cried Princess Bridget.

"My feet won't be able to run and hop and leap anymore. How will I play soccer?"

Princess Bridget sighed and peered through the telescope. This time she didn't watch the children playing soccer. This time, she watched for Miss Posy to arrive.

Miss Posy made her entrance just before teatime.

"Lift your heads up high, stand up straight, keep your shoulders back, stick your chests out, and hold your tummies in!" Miss Posy ordered the royal guards as soon as she arrived.

"Bend from the knees, my man," she told a servant.

Next, Miss Posy marched into the kitchen where the cook was preparing cucumber sandwiches.

"Those crusts don't look straight to me," she said.

At teatime, Miss Posy taught Princess Bridget to sit up straight in her chair, keep her knees together, take dainty bites of her cucumber sandwich, and crook her little finger when she lifted her teacup.

The next day, Miss Posy stuck pictures of footprints on the floor of the Great Hall. Princess Bridget had to walk up and down, placing her feet inside the footprints. Then, to make matters worse, Miss Posy made Princess Bridget do it backwards—this time with three books on her head!

"This will improve your balance," said Miss Posy.

Poor, Fidgety Feet, thought Ryan as he peeked through the keyhole. He hoped things would be better on Thursday when Miss Posy had the day off. Maybe they could get in a game of soccer.

By the time Thursday came, Princess Bridget was behaving in a perfectly princessy way. She sat still at the table when she read.

She held her head high and kept her shoulders back when she walked.

"She isn't leaping and jumping and hopping," the queen whispered to the king as they watched their daughter. "I'm glad we hired Miss Posy."

Princess Bridget and Ryan met in the tower later that day. "I wish I could play soccer," she said, "but I'm not sure I can. My feet have stopped wanting to run and jump and hop and leap. Miss Posy has made me prim and proper."

Teardrops fell from Princess Bridget's eyes onto her very un-fidgety feet.

Later that morning, Princess Bridget got a very strange message from the king. The message said she was to go with Ryan and two royal guards for a royal visit. She was surprised when they ended up at the park.

"You're going to play on my team, Fidgety Feet," said Ryan. He had brought his spare uniform—shoes, socks, a shirt, and a pair of shorts. Princess Bridget hid behind a big tree and changed into them. She knew she should be happy about playing soccer, but all she could think about was her un-fidgety feet.

A nervous Princess Bridget stood in line with the rest of the team on the field. She kept her shoulders back, her chest out, and her tummy in. She didn't wriggle her feet.

"I'm not sure if my feet want to kick the soccer ball," she whispered to Ryan.

But when the whistle blew, her feet *did* run and jump and hop and leap. They *wanted* to kick the soccer ball. They *did* kick the ball. First, her left foot kicked it into the goal. Then, her right foot kicked it into the goal! The crowd cheered when Princess Bridget's team won the game.

GOAL!

Bridget cheered, too, and let
her fidgety feet jump up and
down with joy.

After the game, the manager of the kingdom's top soccer team came up and shook Princess Bridget's hand.

"You can run and jump and hop and leap and kick," he said. "But you also have discipline and control. All those things make a good soccer player."

Then he said, "I'd like you to play for our team. Our practices are every Thursday. The coach will see your parents tomorrow to arrange it."

Princess Bridget grinned from ear to ear. "I'd love to be on the team!" *And Thursdays are perfect,* she thought.

"It's a good thing Miss Posy has Thursdays off," Princess Bridget told Ryan on the way back to the palace. "I know she taught me how to stop fidgeting, but I'm sure she'd think that playing soccer is a very unprincessy thing to do."

The next day, the king summoned his daughter.

"Bridget," he said, "how would you like to play on the top soccer team? Practice is every Thursday."

"I'd love to!" said Princess Bridget.

"Now," said the king, "I'd like you to meet the coach."

Princess Bridget could not believe her eyes. "M-miss Posy?!"

The king laughed, "I told you Miss

Posy would know
what to do about fidgety feet."

"Are you ready for practice, Princess Bridget?" asked Coach Posy.
"I thought we could do some drills in the Royal Gardens. Tower rooms
aren't the best place to play soccer!"

Princess Bridget laughed. "Am I ready? Just look at my fidgety feet!"

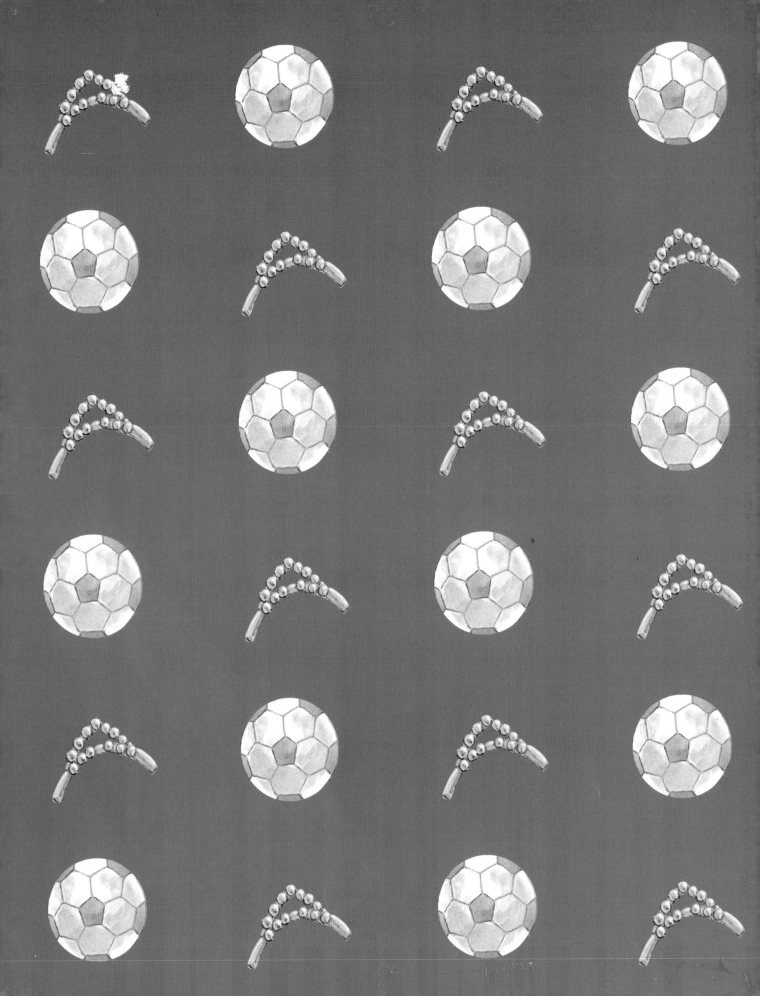